GROUNDWOOD BOOKS
HOUSE OF ANANSI PRESS
TORONTO   BERKELEY

ROOSTER

translation by Elisa Amado
traducción de

GALLO

by
por **Jorge Luján**

pictures by
ilustrado por **Manuel Monroy**

For John Oliver Simon and Rebecca Parfitt with much love JL
To Fernanda, Emilio, Sebastián and Jorgito with all my love MM

Para John Oliver Simon y Rebecca Parfitt con mucho cariño JL
Con todo mi amor para Fernanda, Emilio, Sebastián y Jorgito MM

Groundwood Books / House of Anansi Press
groundwoodbooks.com

With the participation of the Government of Canada
Avec la participation du gouvernement du Canada | Canadä

Library and Archives Canada Cataloguing in Publication
Luján, Jorge, author
Rooster = Gallo / by Jorge Luján ; pictures by Manuel Monroy ; translation by Elisa Amado.
First published in 2004.
Text in English and Spanish.
ISBN 978-1-55498-936-2 (paperback).
— ISBN 978-1-55498-956-0 (pdf)
1. Roosters—Juvenile poetry. I. Amado, Elisa, translator
II. Monroy, Manuel, illustrator III. Luján, Jorge. Gallo.
English. IV. Luján, Jorge. Gallo. Title. V. Title. VI. Title: Gallo.
PZ73.E44Ro 2016   j861'.7   C2016-902478-4

Design by Michael Solomon
Printed and bound in Malaysia

El gallo abre su pico
The rooster opens its beak

y sale el sol.

and up comes the sun.

El sol abre su mano

The sun opens its hand

y nace el día.

and the day is born.

El día se asombra
cuando la noche

The day is surprised when night

tiende su capa
y la colma de estrellas

spreads its cloak and fills it with stars

para que coma el gallo

that the rooster can eat

y vuelva transparente
and so clear the sky

al nuevo día.

for a new day.

El gallo abre su pico
y sale el sol.
El sol abre su mano
y nace el día.
El día se asombra cuando la noche
tiende su capa y la colma de estrellas
para que coma el gallo
y vuelva transparente
al nuevo día.

The rooster opens its beak
and up comes the sun.
The sun opens its hand
and the day is born.
The day is surprised when night
spreads its cloak and fills it with stars
that the rooster can eat
and so clear the sky for
a new day.